Mr Crocodile's cooking class

Dianne Ellis

Illustrations by Janet Davies

Published by Brolga Publishing Pty Ltd
ABN 46 063 962 443
PO Box 12544
A'Beckett St
Melbourne, VIC, 8006
Australia

email: markzocchi@brolgapublishing.com.au

Copyright © 2017 Dianne Ellis
National Library of Australia
Cataloguing-in-Publication data
Ellis, Dianne (author)
Mr Crocodile's cooking class
ISBN: 9780648150817

A catalogue record for this
book is available from the
National Library of Australia

Printed in China

For Mia Rose ... with love

"I would love to be able to cook a sponge cake,"
said Mr Crocodile.

"You should go to cooking classes,"
said Mrs Crocodile.

"Me ... go to cooking classes?"

"If you want to learn to cook,
you should try it," she replied.

Mr Crocodile thought about it and decided to enrol in cooking lessons.

"I want to cook a big double sponge cake," he told Chef at his first class.

"Well, Mr Crocodile, first you have to learn how to cook a simple dish like an oyster omelette," replied Chef.

Mr Crocodile listened to Chef's instructions but his omelette stuck to the pan. There was a lot of smoke in the kitchen.

The other students chuckled.

Mr Crocodile felt embarrassed.

When Mr Crocodile went home, he said to
Mrs Crocodile, "No-one else in the class
burnt their omelette."

"Keep trying. Don't give up.
It's only your first lesson," she replied.

Mr Crocodile practised cooking oyster omelettes at home until they were light and slimy ... just the way he liked them.

At the next lesson, Chef announced they would learn to cook sand-fly scones.

"That sounds easy," Mr Crocodile said.

He listened to Chef's instructions but his scones turned out very hard. They were so hard that Mr Crocodile could bounce his scones off the wall like cricket balls.

The other students laughed out loud.

Mr Crocodile was disappointed.

When Mr Crocodile went home, he said to
Mrs Crocodile, "No-one else's scones in the class
turned out to be cricket balls."

"Don't give up. Keep trying.
It's only your second lesson."

Mr Crocodile practised making sand-fly scones
at home until they were soft and delicious
with a touch of grittiness ...
just the way he liked them.

At the next lesson, Chef announced they would learn to cook mangrove meringue pie.

"Yum! I love mangrove meringue pie," said Mr Crocodile.

He listened to Chef's instructions but he beat the eggs and sugar so hard that the meringue floated up to the ceiling.

The other students rolled on the floor laughing.

Mr Crocodile was angry.

When Mr Crocodile went home, he said to
Mrs Crocodile, "No-one else's meringue mixture
landed on the ceiling."

"Don't give up. Keep trying.
When you practise what you've learnt,
you always succeed."

Mr Crocodile practised making mangrove meringue pies until his meringues peaked perfectly ... just the way he liked them.

At the final cooking lesson, Chef announced they would make a double-layered seaweed sponge cake.

'I really want my cake to turn out perfect,' thought Mr Crocodile.

He followed the instructions carefully and at the end of class, Mr Crocodile received Chef's Award for the tastiest seaweed sponge cake ever!

The other students congratulated him.

Mr Crocodile felt very proud.

When Mr Crocodile went home,
he continued practising all the things he'd
learnt at cooking classes.

He even tried some new recipes and
practised them too. Then he invited his
friends for lunch.

"I approve of these barramundi burgers,"
said Chef.

"These periwinkle pizzas are scrumptious," remarked Mrs Crocodile.

"This mud-crab mousse is heavenly," said Toby Turtle.

"I love the taste of these clam cupcakes," said Christine Cassowary.

"I must have another piece of this yummy seaweed cake," said Sheldon the Shark.

"The food is delicious," his friends chorused.

"What's your secret?" asked Toby.

Mr Crocodile replied, "Practice makes perfect," and he gave Mrs Crocodile a big toothy grin.